How do I use th

Key Words with Peter and Jane has three
parallel series, each containing twelve books. All three
series are written using the same carefully controlled
vocabulary. Readers will get the most out of **Key Words** with
Peter and Jane when they follow the books in the pattern
1a, 1b, 1c; 2a, 2b, 2c and so on.

• Series a
gradually introduces and repeats new words.

• Series b
provides further practice of these same words, but
in a different context and with different illustrations.

• Series c
uses familiar words to teach **phonics** in a methodical way,
enabling children to read increasingly difficult words.
It also provides a link to writing.

LADYBIRD BOOKS

UK | USA | Canada | Ireland | Australia
India | New Zealand | South Africa

Ladybird Books is part of the Penguin Random House group of companies
whose addresses can be found at global.penguinrandomhouse.com.

www.penguin.co.uk   www.puffin.co.uk   www.ladybird.co.uk

First published 1964
This edition 2009, 2014, 2016
Copyright © Ladybird Books Ltd, 1964
001

A CIP catalogue record for this book is
available from the British Library

ISBN: 978-1-409-30135-6

Printed in China

Key Words

with Peter and Jane

10a Adventure on the island

written by W. Murray
illustrated by J.H. Wingfield

Peter and Jane have a rich uncle who has come to live near them. The rich uncle has two boys who are their cousins. The cousins are a lot older than Peter and Jane but they are all very good friends together.

This uncle has just bought an island not far away, and the brother and sister are going to see it. They have a letter from their cousins about the island.

Jane says, " I am glad they live near us now, and that the island is near. It must be nice to be so rich that you can buy an island."

" I am glad our cousins are older than we are," says Peter. " We can be with them when they do interesting things."

" When can we go to see the island?" asks Jane. They read the letter over again to find out. " They say next week," she says. " That is not long to wait."

" It is too long for me," says her brother. " I just can't wait to get there. Won't it be fun when we explore the island? I want to make a camp there after we have had a good look round."

At last the day has come for Peter and Jane to go to their uncle's island for the first time. Their father has brought them to the pier by car to wait for their cousins.

The children go to look at the boats. Some are in the water and others are on the sands. There are little boats, big ones and one very large one. Men are at work on some of the boats. One man is at the water's edge, pulling his boat out of the sea on to the sands.

Another man has turned a little boat over to paint it. Peter and Jane go over to watch him. Peter goes too near the wet paint and gets some on his clothes. The man shows him how to get it off. Jane helps Peter and then says, "There, the paint has gone. You can't see any of it now. Keep away from the wet paint."

They go down to the water's edge to look out to sea. "You can just see the island from here," says Jane. "It won't be long now before we are there. The two boys will be here soon."

As the children come back from the water they see their two cousins get out of a small car. It is their mother's car and she lets them drive it because they both drive very well.

The names of the two big boys are John and Simon. Peter and Jane and their father are happy to see them again. They all talk together for a while and then Father drives home by himself. He knows that John and Simon will look after Peter and Jane and not let them get into danger.

John and Simon pull a small boat down to the water's edge and tell Jane and Peter to get into it. Then the two big boys push the boat into the water and climb in.

John rows the small boat and, as he rows, his brother Simon talks to Peter and Jane. He says, " We are going to row out to our motor boat. It isn't a very large boat but it will take us to the island."

Jane says, " Isn't it fun ! Do we take the little boat with us?"

" Yes," says Simon. " We pull it along behind the motor boat."

In a little while they come to the motor boat, which is tied to a red buoy. Simon holds the boats together as John helps his two cousins into the motor boat. Then the two older boys also climb in.

Simon goes to the engine. He likes to work the engine. Jane and Peter watch as he gets it ready.

Soon John has tied the little boat behind the large one and has made the motor boat ready to move off.

The motor boat starts to move slowly along past the red buoy and past the pier. Simon then makes the boat go more quickly towards the island.

As the motor boat goes along, Peter and Jane look round inside it. It has plenty of room for them all and they can move about if they want to do so. Simon asks them not to move around until they get used to the boat.

They look back at the pier. It is a long way away now. Then they look towards the island. It is not far away.

" I can see a red and yellow buoy," says Peter.

" Yes," says John, " we are making for that buoy."

Simon turns off the engine as the motor boat comes close to the island. The engine slows down and stops, but the boat moves on slowly towards the buoy.

When the buoy is very close Simon takes hold of it and stops the boat. Soon the boys have tied the motor boat to the buoy. Then they get the small boat ready to row to the shore.

They are very close to the shore now and it does not take long to row there. As the small boat takes them across the water, Peter asks if there is anyone else on the island.

" There is nobody else here," says John. " In days gone by, some people used to live here but they have left. The houses they used to live in are here but they are very old."

" Why did the people go away?" asks Jane. John says, " There was no work for them to do on the island, so they could not get any money. Also it was too far to go across to the mainland to work."

" There are plenty of trees and water on the island," says Simon.

" It is going to be fun when we explore," says Peter.

The motor boat has been tied to the buoy, and the small boat is on the beach by the water's edge.

Peter and Jane and their two cousins sit on the sands by their boat for a while. The sky is blue and the sun is hot. " We can bathe from this beach," says Simon. " There is no danger here as the water is not deep close to the shore." The two big boys have been to the island before.

Peter and Jane do not want to bathe in the sea. They want to look over the island first. " We can come back here to bathe this afternoon," says Peter. He soon gets the cousins to show them round.

" Let us go to the top of the hill first," says Simon. " We can see nearly all the island from there. That is why we have our summer house there."

They go across the shore together. Then they walk up the hill. Simon walks first and Peter and Jane come next, with John behind them.

As they go, John tells the brother and sister about the summer house.

" I do hope we can come here many times," says Jane.

They look down from the hill. Below them they can see their motor boat tied to the red and yellow buoy. The little boat is on the beach not far from it.

A little stream of water flows through the woods down to the sea below. Jane says, " I would like to walk by that stream as it flows down to the sea. It looks very beautiful."

Peter looks across to the mainland. He says, " I can see across to the mainland. Could you swim across, John?" He knows that his two cousins can swim very well.

" I don't know," answers John. " It is a long way to swim to the mainland. Simon and I might try to do it one day. There would have to be a boat with us if we did try."

" Father used to swim a lot when he was a young man," says Simon. " He could swim a long way when he was as young as we are. We will talk to him about it."

" Do you want to go down to bathe now?" asks Jane.

" No," answers John. " We will show you the summer house first. We are nearly there."

One of the rooms in the summer house has a very large window which faces the mainland. There is a telescope in the room.

The children and their cousins come into the room, and Simon shows Peter and Jane how to use the telescope. They use it for some time and then John and Simon show the other two round the house.

" There is a large rocket in one of the rooms," John says. " The rocket is for use in time of danger. If the rocket were sent up after dark, people on the mainland would see it and would come to the island to help. The rocket would not show up so well if sent up during the day."

" Father has had some clothes sent here for our use during the holiday," says Simon. " There are some fishing rods in this cupboard and some tins of food. The food keeps a long time when it is in tins."

" We can go on the roof," says Simon. " Come on, I will show you the way up. I will take the telescope up there."

Soon they are all on the roof of the summer house. There is no danger there.

" Let's go to the beach now," says Simon. " We can go down the hill another way to make it more interesting."

" Yes," says Jane, " I want to go down by the stream."

The four of them are soon walking along by the side of the little stream as it flows down to the sea. The sun is shining through the trees on to the children and the water.

They come to a place where they have to get across to the other side of the stream. John and Simon can jump across the water but it is too far for Peter and Jane to jump. The two big boys say that they will make a bridge for their cousins. They find a long log to use as a bridge. When they have put it into place across the stream, John tries it out by going over it first. Then he tells the two young children to walk over the bridge that he and his brother have made.

" Don't be afraid," he says. Peter and Jane are not afraid. The water is not deep and it is not far if they should fall. They walk across the log easily and do not fall.

The stream becomes deeper as they get nearer to the shore.

" We should have brought the fishing rods," says Simon to John as he looks down into the water. " There are quite a lot of fish about."

" Yes," says his brother, " then we could have had fish for tea."

They come to the beach again. As they all want to bathe they change their clothes behind some rocks.

The two big boys are soon swimming easily in the water. Simon swims out to the motor boat. John does not go far from Peter and Jane. The two young children are in the water close to the shore.

" Don't go out too far," says Jane to Peter. " It isn't deep here but it becomes deeper as you get further out."

" The water is quite warm," says Peter. " Yes," says Jane, " the sun has been shining on it all day."

Simon swims back from the motor boat with a large ball. They all play with it in the water.

After the game John and Simon pull their little boat down from the beach into the water. They take turns to climb into the boat and dive out of it.

After they have been swimming for some time the sun goes in and the sky becomes dark.

" It looks like rain," says Simon. " Let's get out of the water."

As they all come out of the water to put on their clothes it starts to rain.

" It gets darker and darker," says John. " We are going to have a storm. Get ready quickly."

But the storm starts too quickly for them. The rain comes down heavily and by the time they have put on their clothes they are all wet through.

" Come on," calls Simon, " we must get out of this. Make for the summer house." They all run up the hill. As they go the thunder and lightning start.

The rain comes down more heavily. There is more thunder and lightning. Simon and John keep close to Peter and Jane as they run.

" Don't be afraid," calls out John. " We are nearly there."

" We're not afraid," says Peter. " This is fun."

" Keep going quickly," says Simon.

At last they get to the summer house. They are so wet it looks as if they have been swimming in the sea in their clothes.

When they get inside the house Peter and Jane start to laugh. " We have never been wet through like this before," says Peter. " It does seem funny," says Jane, " I feel like a fish."

" It won't seem funny if we all get colds," says Simon. " We must get dry." He goes to the cupboard. " I am glad we have had some other clothes brought here," he says.

Soon they are all dry again, and have put on some of the holiday clothes. These are too big for Jane and Peter. " I do feel funny in these," says Peter. " So do I," says Jane, " but it doesn't feel cold."

" No, it doesn't seem cold," says John, " but I think we ought to have a fire to dry the clothes."

The two big boys start a fire in the large room. They all sit round it. The rain comes down heavily outside and they can hear and see the thunder and lightning. " It's a real storm," says Peter. " We must keep inside until it is all over," says Simon.

" I can cook," says Jane. "Would you like me to make you some tea and get you something to eat ?"

" Yes, please," say the boys.

Simon helps Jane to get something to eat and drink. " It doesn't take long to make tea," she says to her cousin.

" I didn't know someone as young as you could cook," says Simon. " Where did you learn? Was it at school?"

" No," answers Jane, " we don't learn to cook at school until we are older. I learn from my mother. I help her quite often, and she shows me what to do. I like to try anything."

They both look into the cupboard for some food. " We have some tea, and some tins of milk, soup and biscuits," says Simon.

" Is there anything else?" asks Jane. " There are a few other tins," answers Simon. " Let us have tea and biscuits, or hot soup. That will do for now."

He opens two of the tins for Jane to get the soup ready. Then Simon opens a tin of biscuits. He lets Jane do nearly all the work because he knows she likes to do it.

When it is all ready they call the other two. " Here it is," says Simon. " Come and get it."

They are all glad to have something hot to drink.

When they have had the tea and biscuits, and the soup, they go to the large window to look out. There is no more thunder or lightning and the rain has nearly stopped.

They wait until the rain has stopped. Then Peter says, " The storm has gone and the rain has stopped. What do we do now?"

" Look down there," says John, " I can't see the motor boat. Where is it?"

" Look further out," says Simon. " Look further out to sea. The motor boat is a long way out and the buoy has gone !"

" Where is the little boat?" asks Jane. " We didn't pull it out of the water when the storm came. The storm made us forget !"

" There it is !" calls out Peter. " I can see our little boat. It is over there by the rocks. It looks damaged to me. The storm has smashed our little boat !"

" If the small boat is smashed we can't get out to the motor boat," says Simon. " We may have to swim out to it, and it looks a long way out."

" There might be danger," says John. " While we were swimming out there the storm might come back."

They take turns to look through the telescope at the two boats.

" The small boat seems badly smashed," says Simon, "I don't think we'll be able to do anything with it."

" There is something wrong with the motor boat," says John. " I think it has a lot of water in it. We may not be able to start the engine if there is too much water in the boat."

" Let's go down to the beach to see what we can do," says Simon.

" Yes," says Jane. " The sun is shining again."

When they get to the beach, they walk over to the rocks to look at their small boat. Its sides are badly damaged where they have hit the rocks.

" We will not be able to do anything about this," says John. " It is too badly damaged."

" We can't get back to the mainland until we have the motor boat," says Peter.

" It's not much use having the motor boat if there is something wrong with the engine," says Simon.

" We must find out about that," John says. " We must swim out to the motor boat or else go out to it on a raft of logs."

Simon and John decide to make a small raft. " We'll be able to make one quickly," says Simon.

" There is plenty of wood about," says John. " I saw some logs in the woods as we came down." He goes back to the summer house for a saw and some rope.

Peter and Jane want to help with the raft so they decide to get logs from the woods. They pull some logs down to the beach where Simon starts to make the raft. " Isn't it exciting?" Jane says to Peter. " We said it would be exciting on the island."

John saws some logs and Simon ties them together with rope to make the raft. Then they make two paddles while their two cousins watch.

When they have made the raft and the paddles the two big boys pull the raft into the water. Then they get ready to go out to the motor boat.

John sits on the raft to paddle it along. Simon swims behind to push.

Peter and Jane are on the shore. Then Peter says, " Come on, we'll go up to the summer house and watch them through the telescope."

They turn and run up the hill together.

As John paddles the raft out to sea he hopes that there is not much wrong with the motor boat.

" Do you think the boat will be badly damaged?" he asks as Simon swims along behind the raft.

" I hope not," says Simon. He does not want to talk much as he finds it hard work to push the raft. " I'll have a turn at swimming in a little while, when you are tired," says his brother.

It does not look as though the storm will come back. The sun is shining and the sky is blue again.

Peter and Jane are now in the summer house. They watch the raft through the telescope. Jane says, " There is not so much danger now that the boys have a raft. If they get tired they can both sit on the raft. They can both paddle if they want to."

After some time the raft comes to the motor boat. Simon ties the two together and then gets into the boat. There is a lot of water in it. " We'll have to get some of this water out," says Simon. The boys decide to do this before they look at the engine.

After they have got most of the water out of the motor boat, Simon says, " I'll have a look at the engine now."

He tries to start it, but he can't make the engine work. He tries again and again but the engine will not start.

John has a go, but he does no better. Then the boys try to dry the engine. They think it will not work because it is wet. However, although they work hard, they can't make it start.

" We are having no luck with this," says Simon. They decide to pull the boat back to the shore with the raft.

Both boys get on the raft and each uses a paddle. They find it hard work to move the motor boat along. However, they are both strong.

Peter and Jane see their cousins start back towards the shore. " Look," says Peter, " they are going to pull the motor boat with the raft. That means they can't start the engine. What bad luck."

" They will get tired pulling that heavy boat," says Jane.

" Yes," says her brother. " It's a heavy boat but the boys are strong. They will be able to bring the boat in."

The two children leave the summer house to go down to the beach. They stand by the water's edge to watch their two cousins paddle the raft along. Although they work hard, their raft moves slowly as it pulls the motor boat after it.

At last the raft comes to the shore and the big boys jump off it. John helps Simon to pull it up on the shore. Peter says to Jane, " We can't just stand here. Let's help John to pull the motor boat out of the water." The big boys do most of the work but they are glad to have the children's help as the motor boat is so heavy.

When part of the big boat rests on the sands, Simon and John try again to start the engine. Again they have no luck, and Simon says, " It's no use. It's getting darker now. It looks as though we'll have to stay on the island all night."

" How exciting !" says Jane.

" You are not afraid, then?" asks Simon.

" No, of course not," answers Jane.

" We must leave the boat here," says John. " Let's go up to the house now."

They all start to walk up the hill once more.

They all go into the summer house to rest and to talk. They are getting tired now. The sun has gone down and it is darker.

"Our mothers and fathers will worry if we don't get home soon," says Simon. "We were going to be home by dark."

"Yes," says John, "I think we should light a fire outside, on the top of the hill. It would have to be a very big fire to be seen on the mainland."

Simon says, "We could send up that rocket we have in the other room." They all decide to do this.

Jane gets ready to stay the night in the summer house, while the boys go outside to light the fire and send up the rocket. It is quite dark now.

It does not take long to get ready. They light the fire first so that they can see by it. They make a very big fire so that it can be seen a long way away. When it is going well they have to stand back as it is so hot.

Then Simon says he is going to light the rocket. He makes the others keep away as he does so.

Simon lights the rocket and then stands back. " Stand back," he says to the others. " It will go up now." They watch the rocket. Jane looks out of the window of the house.

Then the rocket goes off. It shoots up into the night sky. As it goes it lights up part of the island. For a few minutes they can see all around them. Then all is dark again.

" Well, that's that! " says John. " I hope they saw it on the mainland."

" Don't worry," says Simon. " I'm sure they must have seen it. All we can do now is wait."

" Yes," says Peter, " We'll wait and see."

They go into the house again. They find that Jane has been busy getting some hot soup ready for them. " Come on," she says, " I'm sure you will like this. There is a big fire to sit by while you have it."

" You have been busy, Jane," says John.

They sit around the fire, as they have their soup. Then they talk for a few minutes.

"I am not going to bed for a while," says Simon. " You can all go when you want to. Don't worry, someone will come to get us soon."

Simon rests by the fire while the others sleep. They sleep in the clothes they have on. Their own clothes are not quite dry from the storm.

Now and again Simon goes outside to see if he can hear or see anything. He thinks that a boat might come for them at any time. However, no boat comes and after a long while Simon feels so tired he goes to sleep. When he wakes up it is morning.

John wakes up and comes in to see Simon. " So no boat came during the night," he says.

" No," says his brother. " It will come this morning, I feel sure."

" We must have some food," says John. " I'm going to wash, and then catch some fish."

" Our own clothes are dry now," says Simon. " We can put them on again." They have a wash and put on their own clothes. Then John takes a fishing rod and goes to the stream.

A few minutes later, Peter and Jane wake up. They wash and put on their own dry clothes. Simon tells them that John has gone to catch some fish. Peter goes to find him, and Simon and Jane look through the telescope.

John is able to catch three fish from the stream. He lets Peter use the fishing rod to catch one more.

" Now we have four, so that is one each for breakfast," says John.

They take the fish to the house and help Jane to cook the breakfast.

After breakfast they take turns to look through the telescope towards the mainland. Simon watches first, while the others go down to the beach for a bathe.

" It's a lovely day," says Jane to Peter. " I don't think a storm will catch us as we bathe today."

After their swim they go back to the house. As John is taking his turn at the telescope he calls out, " A boat is coming ! A boat is coming towards the island !"

" How exciting !" says Jane. " Can you see who is in it ?"

" No, I have tried, but it is too far away," answers her cousin. " The people in the boat look so small I can't see who they are."

They all look through the telescope one after another. After a few minutes Simon calls out, " It is Father ! He has two other men with him but I don't know them."

The boat is coming close to the island now.

Peter and Jane and their cousins run quickly down to the beach.

" I'm glad you are all safe," calls out the boys' father from his big boat as it comes in to the shore.

" Yes, we are all safe and well," says Simon, " but both of our boats have been damaged."

The three men soon get out of their boat on to the shore, and Simon and John tell them what the storm did to their own two boats. The men have a look at the damage and then decide to pull the boys' motor boat back to the mainland behind their big boat.

The boys' little boat has been too badly damaged to be put into the water, so they put it into the boys' motor boat. Then they all push this motor boat into the sea and tie it behind their big boat.

The men tell the children to jump in and soon they move away from the island.

" We tried not to worry about you, but we did," says the father to his two boys. Then he says to Peter and Jane, " Your mother and father have come to our house. They will be glad to see that you are safe."

New words used in this book

Page

Page

4   rich near cousins
older island

6   brought large
edge gone

8   drive John Simon
rows isn't behind

10   tied buoy engine
move starts past
towards around

12   close shore
across else
mainland

14   beach bathe
nearly

16   below stream
flows answers
might try young

18   telescope rocket
sent during fishing
rods tins food

20   let's side shining
bridge afraid
easily

22   becomes quite
swimming further

24   darker storm
heavily thunder
lightning

26   seem funny feel
colds dry doesn't

28   didn't anything
soup biscuits few

30   stopped damaged
smashed

32   badly we'll able
wrong raft

34   decide exciting
ties paddles

36   hard I'll tired
though

38   most however
although luck
strong heavy

40   leave stand rests
getting stay

42   worry light seen
send

44   minutes I'm
sure busy

46   sleep wakes
wash catch

48   breakfast coming
tried

50   safe

Total number of new words: 115
Average repetition per word: 8